June. 18 - 1944

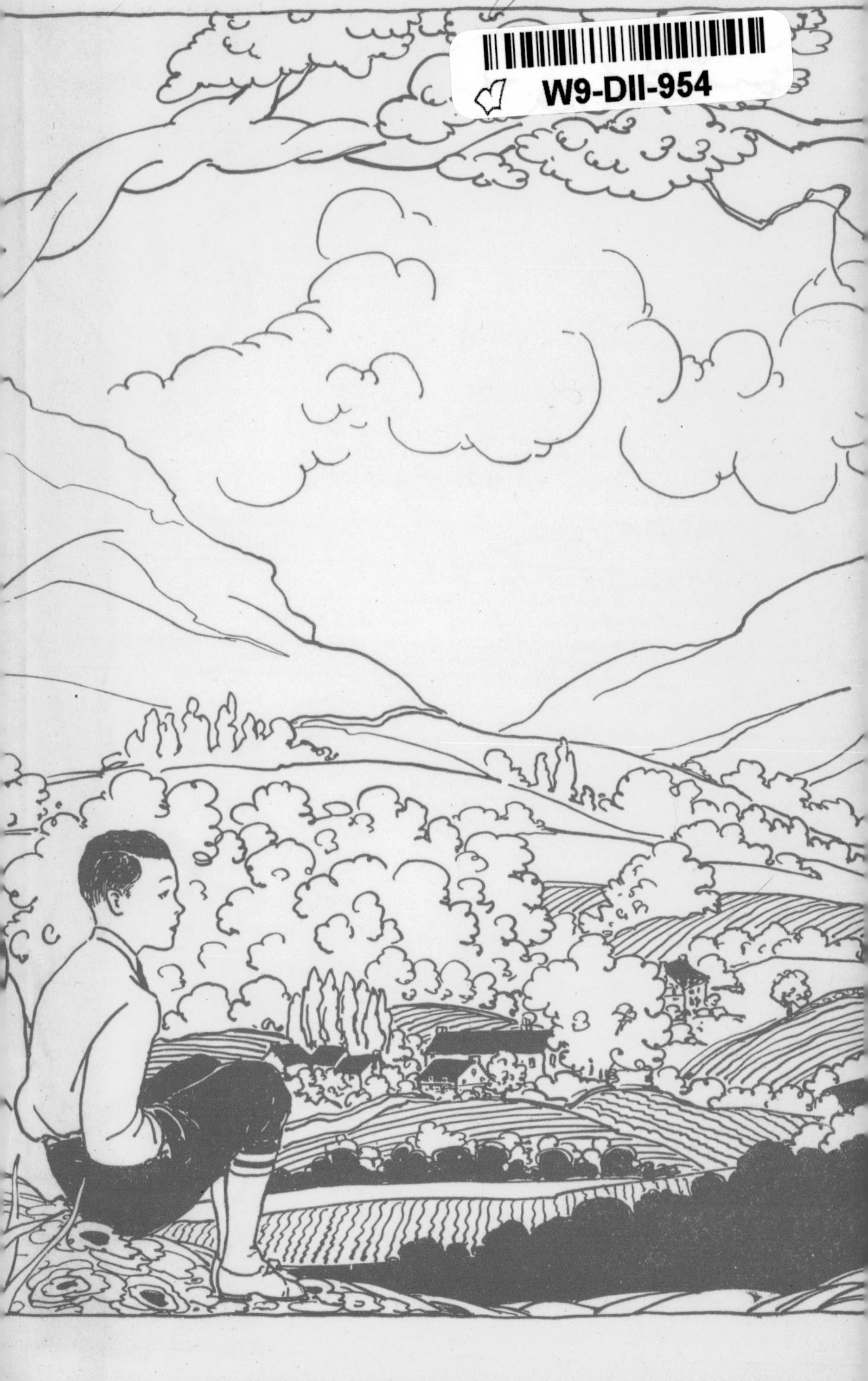

LITTLE TOM
OF ENGLAND

PEMBROKE CASTLE

LITTLE TOM
of ENGLAND

BY
MADELINE BRANDEIS

Photographic Illustrations

 This book, while produced under wartime conditions, in full compliance with government regulations for the conservation of paper and other essential materials, is
COMPLETE AND UNABRIDGED

GROSSET & DUNLAP
PUBLISHERS   NEW YORK
by arrangement with the A. Flanagan Company

DEDICATION
To a Sincere Scholar and Lover of Books

THOSE WHO POSED FOR THE ILLUSTRA-
TIONS IN "LITTLE TOM OF ENGLAND"

TOM..DAVID TILLOTSON
BOB...JAMES HOYT
MRS. BENTLEY..............................GERALDINE STERN
HARKNESS...................................EDGAR NORTON

THOSE WHO READ AND HELPFULLY CRITI-
CIZED "LITTLE TOM OF ENGLAND"

MR. AND MRS. CRAUFURD KENT
AND
MR. JAMES GERSTLEY

To You, My Good Friends, Deepest Thanks!

CONTENTS

LITTLE TOM OF ENGLAND MAKES FRIENDS WITH LITTLE
BOB OF AMERICA

Little Tom of England

CHAPTER I

"THE LITTLE ANGEL"

"Sissy!"

Bob threw down his beautiful book. Threw it down hard. The neat, colored jacket came off and slid across the cabin floor. The picture on the jacket stared up reproachfully at Bob.

It was the picture of stout, rosy-cheeked John Bull, who represents Great Britain, just as Uncle Sam represents the United States. The name of the book was "Young England."

Bob climbed upon his berth and looked sadly out of the cabin porthole. The sea was green pea soup; furious green pea soup! The ship was rolling; the wind shrieked.

Bob turned to the other berth, where a figure lay, silent and still.

"Mother," he said. "Please let me go up on deck. I'm so tired of staying down here in the cabin!"

His mother stirred and opened suffering eyes. They seemed to ask how anyone could possibly feel well enough to want to do anything!

"Why don't you read, Bob?" she asked. "This is your chance to learn about the country you are going to visit. And from such wonderful books, too!"

Bob made a slang remark which was not pretty, but expressed his feelings. Then he looked down at John Bull, sprawling upon the floor and said:

"The boy in that book is a sissy, Mother! I don't want to read about him!"

Whereupon Bob pursed his lips, raised his voice to a squeak, and started to mock the hero of "Young England."

"Oh, I say!" he mim-
icked. "Do bring my
tea, Perkins! Oh,
fancy! I've dropped
a stitch in my knit-
ting! Dear, dear!"

"Bob!" scolded Mrs.
Bentley. "Please don't
mock at things you
know nothing about!

"SISSY"

English boys are as manly as American
boys! Just because their words and expres-
sions are different from yours—"

Her voice trailed off as the sea lifted the
ship up on a wave and let it fall down again.
It felt to Mrs. Bentley much like one of those
sudden dips in an elevator. It did strange
things to her and she groaned.

"Oh, run along, Bob," she sighed. "I'm
too ill to argue with you. But put on your
raincoat, and be careful if you walk on deck.
It's blowing so terribly!"

Bob jumped down eagerly from his bunk. Released at last!

They had left New York yesterday, and today it had been storming since early morning.

Poor mother! Of course, Bob had tried to comfort her. But a ten-year-old boy is as much comfort in a sick room as a playful lion cub!

So Bob's freckled nose now wriggled eagerly as he pulled on his heavy raincoat. He was sniffing adventure like a cat sniffing a mouse.

" 'Bye, Mom," he called. "I'll be back before dinner time."

The door slammed behind him.

How hot and stuffy they kept this old boat! Bob started down the narrow, white hallway, and the ship played football with him. He zigzagged from one side to the other, until he finally reached the stairs.

Up into the spacious lounge, out on to the

OLD YORK MINSTER, THE LARGEST OF THE MEDIEVAL
ENGLISH CATHEDRALS

deck he went. All the steamer chairs were removed, making the deck look like a bare stage without its scenery.

The wind lashed the ship, spray splashed the deck windows, and Bob suddenly felt himself hurled against the rail. He straightened out again and proceeded unsteadily down the promenade.

A lone sailor came walking toward him, body bent like a willow tree.

"Hello!" greeted Bob. "Some storm, isn't it?"

"Rather!" returned the British sailor.

Bob explored the ship. He found little of interest here above. Everyone was below, most of them ill. He visited the gymnasium. Empty! The children's playroom. Empty! The swimming pool. Empty—of swimmers and water.

Then he inspected the second-class quarters.

"Just like first-class," he decided. "Only

a little smaller, and there are no big paintings around. I like it better."

He walked and he walked. What a huge city to call itself a ship!

At last Bob found himself in a strange world of dark passageways and steamy, close air. He was in the lowest part of the vessel—in the quarters of those who ran it!

Bob knew that he had no right to be here. He had passed two "No Admittance" signs without anyone's seeing him do it. So here he was, where the real people of the ship lived—those who made it go!

He must be close to the engine room. It was terribly hot. Bob poked his nose into one dark corner after another. Hello! Here was a big cabin, crowded with bunks.

Nobody seemed to be in there now. Bob entered. He glanced around and thought he saw a figure lying on the bunk at the far end of the room.

He started in that direction, when the ship

suddenly gave him a mighty shove. He found himself standing beside the bunk, looking down at a boy who was reading.

The boy's knees made a mountain in front of him, on which rested an open book. He did not look up, even at Bob's abrupt appearance.

"Hello," said Bob. "I nearly landed on top of you. What a storm this is!"

Bob smiled his broad, one-tooth-gone smile and waited for an answer. But the reading boy read on.

"Say!" Bob raised his voice. "Didn't you hear me? I said, 'Hello'!"

"Oh, hello!" responded the boy, without raising his head. He went right on reading.

Bob was growing angry. Who did this boy think he was, anyway, to act so high and mighty? And living down here in the bowels of the boat, too! Nervy brat!

Swish! Over on its side went the ship! The walls creaked as if they were to be torn apart. Things rattled and squeaked. The reading boy was thrown out of his bunk and lay upon the floor.

He pushed his yellow locks out of his eyes and looked up at Bob. His eyes were very blue and wide and full of amazement. Where, thought Bob, had he seen this boy before?

"How did I get on the floor?" asked the lad. "Do you know?"

Bob started to reply, when the boat thought it a good time for another spin. The boy on the floor was rolled over in a heap. When he sat up again he groaned. Bob bent over him.

"Are you hurt?" he asked.

"No, I think not," responded the other boy.

He arose and threw himself on the bunk, passing his hand over his eyes as he did so.

"Are you seasick?" Bob asked.

The boy looked through his fingers and

"OH, I SAY!"

smiled. He had dimples in his cheeks, but
his teeth were a bit crooked.

"Oh, I say!" he laughed. "As a matter of
fact, I am!"

Then, before Bob could speak, the boy
raised himself on his elbow and continued,
"You know, I've been feeling rotten ever
since we left New York! But I wouldn't let
on. Not I! Fancy admitting it to those—"

He broke off. "But, I say!" he laughed again, "Why am I telling you this? Who are you? At first I thought you were one of those beastly page boys, and I wouldn't bother to look up from my book. They rag me so, because I'm younger than they are. What's your name?"

"Bob Bentley," replied the American. "What's yours?"

"Tom Jenks," said the English lad. "I dare say you're a passenger," he went on, "though I did not notice you at tea yesterday."

Now Bob knew who he was! A page boy! The littlest one! The one whom all the ladies had "oh'd" and "ah'd" over when he had passed the cakes at tea time. He had been dressed in a trim little uniform.

Even Mother had pointed him out and said, "Look, Bob! That fellow can't be any older than you are, and he's earning his living as a ship's page! Poor little chap!"

A bald-headed gentleman had listened to mother and he added, "You know, I think that in the whole of my life I've never seen a homely English child. They're all quite beautiful!"

Another passenger had entered into the conversation and remarked, "That reminds me of a story. Long ago, when the English were known as Angles, Pope Gregory the Great once saw some of them in the Roman Slave Market.

"The Pope said, 'These Angles should be called Angels because they are so fair.'"

Then another lady had gushed, "Oh, this little page does look just like an angel!"

Now, as Bob looked at Tom, sitting up in his bunk, he thought to himself:

"Little angel! Little English angel! With his dimples, his golden hair, and his British accent! I'd like to punch him in the nose!"

CHAPTER II

THE FIGHT

"Would you care to look at my books?" asked Tom.

He was sitting up on the bunk and his blue eyes were shining. Pink spots showed in his cheeks, and Bob imagined that his mother would call the brat beautiful. Doubtless, she would also admire his absurd English accent!

Bob sat at the foot of the bunk, disliking the little page more every minute. Sissy! Just like the kid in his book, "Young England"!

Yet Bob remained. He was fascinated, in spite of himself, by this strange, new creature—an English boy!

Tom wore a faded shirt and a pair of funny-looking trousers, clumsy and thick.

21

His trim page's uniform hung upon a hook on the wall near by. Now he began to pull some worn books from beneath his bunk.

"I'm jolly proud of my books," he said, and opened a large volume over which he bent. "What do you think of my maps? Look at this one of the world. I've been following our course on it ever since we left New York.

"We shall reach England in four days, ten hours, and forty minutes now! I shall be jolly glad to get back to England!"

As Bob gazed at the map, a wicked gleam came into his eye.

"Your England looks like a fly speck on the ocean!" he sneered. "It's just a tiny island, no bigger than New York State!"

But Tom was not in the least dismayed. "Right you are!" he agreed. "And that's just why it's so wonderful to think that England is the most important country in the world!"

"She is not!" cried Bob furiously.

Courtesy Photochrom Co., Ltd., London

BAMBURGH CASTLE, ON THE NORTHUMBERLAND COAST

But Tom calmly went right on talking.
"Just take her great authors," he said.
"Shakespeare, Dickens—"

"Oh, the dickens!" sputtered Bob, and his
fists began to clench together.

"I'll show you what Rudyard Kipling
wrote about England," said Tom, and he began to turn the pages of another book.
"Here it is. He wrote:

" 'Never was isle so little,
      Never was sea so lone
      But over the scud and the palm-trees
      An English flag has flown.'

"That's because," went on the page, "we
own so many countries in every part of the
world. Canada is one of them. Of course
you've heard the saying, 'The sun never sets
on the British Empire.' It's true. There's
not a place in the world where Englishmen
have not settled. They've been great ex-
plorers and discoverers since earliest
times."

Bob was beginning to boil. If this boy made another remark about England, he'd let his fist do what it was tingling to do.

"It's been a whole year since I saw England," said Tom wistfully.

Bob tried hard to control himself.

"Where have you been living?" he asked, not caring very much.

"In New York," replied Tom.

"Why didn't you stay there?" asked Bob. His tone seemed to say, "Wasn't it good enough for you?"

"For one thing," answered Tom, "my mother's in England. And, for another, I shouldn't want to grow up to be an American!"

Bob felt the blood mount to his face and before he knew what had happened, his fist had broken loose. It was then a battle royal between the two boys.

First they rolled upon Tom's bunk. Then they did a bit of rolling on the floor. The

THEY ROLLED ON THE FLOOR

pitching ship helped them roll. In fact, the ship took great pleasure in tossing this nice, large ball made of boy.

They puffed. They panted. Their faces turned lobster red. Their shirts came popping out at the waists. Bob fought as he had never fought before. But he found that his wind was growing less and less and finally he started to gasp.

The ship seemed suddenly to turn a complete somersault, and then all went black in front of Bob.

The next thing he knew, Tom was bending over him, sprinkling cold water in his face.

"Are you all right?" asked the English boy anxiously.

"What happened?" Bob sat up. He found that he had been lying on Tom's bunk.

"We had a bit of a fight," said Tom.

"And you won," added Bob.

The other boy looked uncomfortable for a moment and did not answer. Then he remarked, "I say, hadn't you better be going back to your quarters? It's almost tea time, you know."

Bob noticed that several men had entered the room and had gone to their bunks.

"I'll go," said Bob.

He sat up and began to stuff in his shirt. He felt slightly dizzy, but otherwise all right.

"I'll come back again, though, and have it out with you for what you said!" he flung at Tom.

"What did I say?" asked the little English page. His eyes were wide and innocent.

"About not wanting to be an American!" answered Bob hotly.

Tom laughed. "Why, I didn't mean anything by that!" he said. "I'm frightfully fond of the U.S. But I shouldn't want to risk growing up to be a President or—or— well, you see, I was born English and I shall remain so!"

Bob remembered a song from the opera, "Pinafore":

> "But in spite of all temptations
> To belong to other nations,
> He remains an Englishman."

Tom went on talking. "My father was a seafaring man," he said. "I'm the oldest boy in the family, so he brought me along

with him to America a year ago. He
thought he should make good in New York,
so to speak, and then send for the rest of
the family. But, you see, my father—he
died a fortnight ago."

Bob sat up straight in the bunk. "So did
mine!" he exclaimed. "That's why my
mother came away on this trip. To try to—
forget."

"Oh, I say," remarked Tom. "I *am*
sorry!"

Bob hung his head. He had no words.
But Tom sat down on the bunk and put out
his hand.

"Shall we be friends?" he asked. "You
see, everything I said about England goes
for America as well."

"What do you mean?" inquired Bob.

"Why, it's like this," replied Tom. "England and America have the same history and
heroes. As a matter of fact, England is
home to most Americans, as your ancestors

WARWICK CASTLE

set out from there to discover your country, you know!"

"I never thought of that," said Bob. "But it's true all right!"

"Rather!" agreed Tom. "We're the world's two great English-speaking nations!" Then he smiled and added, "Even though you Americans do talk with an accent!"

"An accent!" cried Bob, and his mouth fell open. "It's you English who have the accent!"

Tom laughed. "That depends upon which country you happen to be in," he answered.

Just then a bell clanged and Tom jumped up.

"Sorry," he said. "I must dress for tea now."

He started to take off his old, worn trousers.

"I look better in my uniform," he said. "These trousers are ever so ugly, I know.

Yet they've done service. And, of course, I do like them, as my father made them for me."

"Your father made them?" squeaked Bob.

"Right!" agreed Tom. "Father was a sailor, you know, and sailors can all sew. Why, he even lined these for me so I should be warm during my first New York winter."

Bob grinned, shuffled his feet, and felt uncomfortable.

But Tom grabbed his hand and gave him a friendly smile.

"Shall you be coming back here to see me?" he asked.

"Tomorrow," said Bob, with a hearty handshake.

CHAPTER III

THE LOCKET

"Mother," called Bob, "may I borrow your locket with Father's picture in it?"

"Why do you want it, Bob?" asked Mrs. Bentley.

"Well, you see," explained Bob, "yesterday, Tom was showing me a picture of his father. So I thought I'd like to show him one of my dad."

It was the last day on board. In a few hours the ship would be at Plymouth. Bob was going below to bid good-bye to his friend.

Mrs. Bentley's eyes filled with tears as she took from her neck an exquisite little locket. The picture of Bob's father was set in a circle of diamonds.

"Be very careful with it, Bob," she said, as she handed the locket to him. "You know how I treasure it.   And hurry back, for we have a great deal to do before we land."

"I will, Mother," promised Bob, and he put the locket into his pocket.

But many days were to pass before that little locket again adorned the neck of Bob's mother—many days filled with danger.

Bob, however, was quite unaware of this as he now whistled his way cheerfully to the bowels of the ship.   Entering Tom's cabin he called:

"Hello, there!   Are you at rest?"

Tom was sitting on his bunk, surrounded by Bob's beautiful books.   His cheeks flamed red and his eyes shone.

Ever since Bob had brought his fine volumes below, the little English boy had had his nose buried in their pages.   And, every day, at rest period, Young America had paid Young England a visit.

So it happened that before Bob Bentley had really known it, he had found himself

TOM READS TO BOB

listening to stories told or read by the en-
thusiastic Tom.

For instance, the little page had said that
the fishing village where his own family
lived was near the birthplace of King
Arthur of the Knights of the Round Table.

He had read to Bob about England's many
bloody wars. About William the Conqueror
who, in the long ago, invaded Britain and

made himself the first Norman king. About Henry the Eighth, with his six wives; and the powerful Queen Elizabeth, known as "Good Queen Bess."

Soon Bob began to look forward to visiting the places where such colorful people had lived. He now thought of London as a story-book city.

He wanted to visit the Tower, where Sir Walter Raleigh was imprisoned and where those two unfortunate little princes were murdered.

He wanted to see where Charles Dickens' stories had taken place, and the home of William Shakespeare. It seemed that every town in England was connected with the name of some great author.

Tom also introduced him to new book adventures—"Kim," "Lorna Doone," "Kenilworth." The day that Bob had begun to read, Mrs. Bentley had dropped her own book and stared at him in amazement.

"No, Mom, I'm not sick!" Bob had laughed. "But, you see, I was all wrong about English boys being sissies. Just because they talk differently doesn't mean that they can't punch!"

And Bob had rubbed his stomach with painful recollections.

Today, as Bob sat down upon Tom's bunk, there was no thought of punches between the two boys. For a great friendship had grown up out of that first fight.

"Look here, Tom," said Bob, holding up the locket with his father's picture in it. "This is my dad."

Tom gazed soberly at the handsome face of Bob's father in its setting of diamonds.

"He *was* a fine gentleman!" exclaimed the page.

Then he pulled out the picture of his own father, who resembled a walrus in a sailor cap. For Thomas Jenks, Senior, had worn long whiskers. The photograph was a cheap, weather-stained affair and Tom eyed the expensive little locket that belonged to Bob's mother.

"I say!" he breathed, "Wouldn't my mother just love to have such a locket to frame father's photo in! I do wish I might bring her one!"

For the first time Bob began to realize about Tom. He must be a very poor boy, else he would not have had to work his way home as a page.

Bob put his hand into his pocket and felt for some money. He had two large bills which his mother had given him yesterday for his birthday. But no! He couldn't offer money to Tom! That would be like tipping him, and they were friends, not master and servant.

"Time we were saying good-bye," declared Tom suddenly. "I must dress. There's a lot to do, you know, before we arrive."

As he spoke, he turned his back to Bob and

stooped down to pick up a book which had
fallen on the floor. And as he stooped, Bob
quickly stuffed the two paper bills into
Tom's trouser pocket.

How old and worn those trousers were!
thought Bob, as he withdrew his hand. Oh,
well, Tom would be able to buy some new
ones when he found the money!

But Bob did not know that his friend
would not find the money! He would not
find it because there was a hole in that
pocket, and the two paper bills had fallen
through this hole, into the lining of the
homemade trousers—fallen down to the
bottom of the leg, where they now lay.

But this was not the worst. For along
with that money had dropped something
else.   A little diamond-studded locket!
Carelessly Bob had pulled his mother's precious locket out of his pocket with the
money! And there it lay at the bottom of
Tom's trouser leg beside the paper bills.

"Here are your books," said Tom, turning around and facing Bob.

"Wouldn't you like to keep one of them?" asked Bob. "Just as a—a reminder of the trip, I mean."

"Oh, no!" laughed Tom. "Thanks awfully, but you'll be wanting them to remind *you* of England, once you're back in America. And do remember," he added, "to look me up, should you get to Clovelly."

"I will," promised Bob. "And don't you forget to write to me. I gave you the name of my hotel in London."

"Right-o!" said Tom.

"So long!" said Bob.

"Cheerio!" called Tom.

CHAPTER IV

THE ARRIVAL

"The cliffs of England stand,
Glimmering and vast, out in the tranquil bay."
—Matthew Arnold

England at last!

Those who were to land at Plymouth were sent to shore in small boats called tenders.

"I feel like a sardine!" laughed Bob.

He and his mother were packed into the tender with a crowd of other Plymouth-bound travellers. A jumble of luggage surrounded them.

"You know, Mom," continued Bob, "Tom said that ships can't land every place on the English shore because it may be too rocky or too shallow or the cliffs too steep."

Mrs. Bentley smiled. She had noticed

41

VIEW OF PLYMOUTH FROM THE TENDER

that most of Bob's sentences began with the words, "Tom said."

"And," went on her son, "Tom said that the old name for England was Albion, which means 'white,' because the cliffs are so white. Did you know that, Mom?"

THE PLYMOUTH HOE

Yes, Mrs. Bentley knew. And she also
knew something else, which was that she felt
a deep gratitude toward the little English
page Tom. For he had succeeded in interesting her son in the country through which
they were soon to travel.

When Bob had told his mother how he had

dropped the money into Tom's pocket, she had been pleased. She had felt that he deserved it.

But Mrs. Bentley had entirely forgotten to ask Bob for her locket. In the confusion of last-minute packing and passport examinations, it had slipped her mind.

They could hear the band on the steamer playing "Rule Britannia." The music stirred a deep pride in Bob's heart. Here was the land of his ancestors! A land of brave men, of learned scholars!

He began to think of Tom, who was a scholar. Tom would soon be on his way to the little fishing village where his family lived.

He had explained to Bob that the chief steward on the boat was an old friend of his father. He had seen to it that Tom should be permitted to leave the ship at Plymouth, for the vessel was to go on to London. He had also given the boy his job on board.

HARKNESS, THE CHAUFFEUR

The tender docked on Plymouth's shores, and Bob shifted his thoughts from Tom Jenks to the Pilgrim Fathers. It was from here that they had sailed to settle America.

The Bentleys were met by a courteous, pleasant-faced chauffeur in a trim, English automobile. He was to take them on a tour through a part of England before finally reaching London. His name was Harkness.

Bob was struck by the many unfamiliar sights and objects around him.

"Look at those funny carts!" he cried. "What do you think they are, Harkness?"

"They are milk prams, Master Robert," explained Harkness.

Yes, they did look like babies' perambulators, or prams, as the English call them.

They walked out to see The Hoe, a promenade on the cliffs. One day, long ago, Sir Francis Drake was bowling on The Hoe, when a messenger rushed up to him, crying:

"The Spanish Armada is approaching!"

But Drake, the fearless explorer, had insisted upon finishing his game of bowls. Then he sailed off to fight and to win his glorious victory over the Spanish fleet.

It was also from this spot that Sir Francis Drake had started out in his "Golden Hind" to circle the world.

A MILK PRAM

Mrs. Bentley was very quiet and sad. She was thinking of the last time she had seen these shores. Her husband had been with her then. Tears came to her eyes and she found it difficult to swallow. She put her hand up to her throat—and missed the locket!

"Bob!" she cried. "Where is my locket? You did not return it to me!"

Bob searched through all his pockets. Of course, the locket was not there!

"I—I can't find it, Mom!" breathed Bob. "It's gone!"

Mrs. Bentley's face was as white as the chalk cliffs of England.

"Oh, Bob, what have you done?" she cried.

"I just took it below to show to Tom, Mother," said the miserable Bob. "And then I put it right back into my pocket."

A strange look came over Mrs. Bentley's face. "You don't think that the page boy—" she began.

"Oh, Mom!" gasped Bob. "Tom wouldn't do anything wrong! I know he wouldn't!"

"I didn't mean that, dear," said Mrs. Bent-

"IT'S GONE!"

ley. "Only, when you took that money out of your pocket to give him, perhaps you pulled out the locket with it."

"Oh, Mom!" Bob's face lit up. "That's just what happened! When I put the money into Tom's pocket, I must have put the locket in, too, by mistake! So, of course, when he finds it, he'll return it to us!"

"Nevertheless," said Mrs. Bentley, "I think I shall report the loss to the ship's purser. Then we'll have a look around Plymouth and see whether we can find Tom."

"I'm sure he's already started for Clovelly, Mom," said Bob. "He told me he could hardly wait to get home."

"In that case," said Mrs. Bentley, "we shall have to follow him to Clovelly and recover my locket before we start on our tour."

They reported their loss to the purser. Then they searched for Tom in Plymouth. But the search was unsuccessful. Tom was already on his way home.

"How far is Clovelly from here, Harkness?" Mrs. Bentley asked the chauffeur.

"Not very far, Madam," beamed the sympathetic Harkness. "As a matter of fact, it's just on the opposite sea coast."

Mrs. Bentley frowned. "That will take us out of our way, won't it?" she asked.

"Oh, not worth mentioning, Madam," purred the chauffeur. "I shouldn't wonder if we could be there soon after tea time if we start at once."

It was as if he had said to a baby, "There now, don't fret. It'll only be a moment until I have your bottle ready!"

"Very well, let us go then," said Mrs. Bentley.

So she and Bob entered the automobile and they started for Tom Jenks' little fishing village on the opposite shore.

But Tom Jenks himself had, it seems, chosen a different road to Clovelly.

He now walked cheerfully along, his hands in his pockets, delighted to be on British soil once again.

He loved the gentle-faced people he saw on the streets, and the purple-cheeked cab drivers with their twinkling eyes.

Tom noticed that boys taller than he still wore short breeches. They stared at him in his long, American-style trousers. But Tom didn't care much. He was too happy.

How should he know that a valuable locket lay at the bottom of his trouser leg, nestled among two paper bills? And how should he know that Bob Bentley and his anxious mother were on their way to Clovelly to recover that locket from him?

As it happened, the Bentleys, in their fast automobile, were to arrive at the home of Tom Jenks long before Tom himself did.

And, strangely enough, the Bentleys were to be the first to hear some startling news which awaited the little page in his native village.

CHAPTER V

THE STARTLING NEWS

Bob Bentley and his mother were on their way to Clovelly. Bob remembered that Tom had said, "No town in England is more than seventy miles from the sea. Of course, this includes the busy rivers and bays."

They had left Plymouth behind and were being driven along narrow, twisting motor roads, with English countryside spread out around them—well-groomed countryside, looking, every bit of it, like some old maid's pampered garden!

They stopped at a filling station.

"I shall need some petrol, Madam," said the chauffeur to Mrs. Bentley.

"What's that?" whispered Bob to his mother.

"Gasoline," she replied.

Courtesy Associated British Railways, Inc.

A VILLAGE NEAR TORQUAY IN SOUTH DEVON

Bob shook his head. "And I thought I understood English!" he muttered.

They decided to lunch at Torquay, a noisy, crowded seaside resort. The lunch consisted of cold roast beef and salad. The waiter asked Bob, "Will you have a sweet, sir?"

"A sweet what?" inquired Bob, puzzled.

Mrs. Bentley came to his rescue.

"A sweet means a dessert," she explained.

After their sweet, they continued on their journey through the toyland of Devonshire.

"What is Devonshire cream, Harkness?" asked Bob. He had once heard the name.

"Oh, it's really the nicest thing you've ever tasted, Master Robert," smiled the driver.

He pronounced "tasted" "tīsted." Mrs. Bentley explained to Bob later that Harkness spoke with a Cockney accent. A Cockney is a person from the ancient part of London.

There is an old church called the Bow Church and it is said that a true Cockney is born within the sound of Bow Bells. By his speech, Bob thought that Harkness must have been born in the very belfry of the church!

A HOUSE IN DEVONSHIRE

When they stopped later for tea, Bob found that the chauffeur had been quite right about Devonshire cream.

A timid little waitress served them in the garden of a roadside cottage. She asked them if they wished a "cream tea" which, it seemed, was a trifle more costly.

The cream was so thick that they spread it on their bread. They also had jam and cakes, and Bob arose feeling like a well-blown-up balloon.

"It's so funny always to have to keep to the left," observed Bob, as the car rolled along once again.

Harkness smiled. "I dare say it must appear odd to you," he agreed. "As a matter of fact, England is one of the few countries where one is obliged to drive to the left."

"When do we reach Bideford?" asked Bob.

It was from Bideford that Sir Richard Grenville, the naval commander, had set sail, many years ago, on his daring sea adventures.

But the chauffeur's face was blank as Bob asked the question.

"I can't say as I've ever 'eard of the place," he answered. "Is it in Hengland?"

Courtesy Associated British Railways, Inc.

ANNE HATHAWAY'S COTTAGE, NEAR STRATFORD

(Harkness robbed words of their "h's," which he gave to other words. For instance, if you will take the "h" away from "Hengland" and give it back to " 'eard," you will understand what he meant!)

"Why, Bideford is right next to Clovelly on the map," said Bob, astonished that Harkness should not know. "It was in Bideford that Charles Kingsley wrote his story, 'Westward Ho!' "

There was a sputter from Harkness. Then the good man turned quite red.

"Oh, I beg pardon, Master Robert," he said. "But I didn't know you meant Bideford!" (Harkness pronounced it "Biddyford" whilst Bob had been making it rhyme with "Side-ford.")

Now it was Bob's turn to flush. He was to find out that words are not always what they seem in England, at least, not to Americans. For instance, "Marjoribanks" is pronounced "Marchbanks," and "Cholmondeley" is "Chumley."

They approached the town of "Westward Ho." Bob wondered whether Harkness would call it "Wahoo," "Whitefish," or merely "Waps." But all he did was to re-

THE CHAUFFEUR'S FACE
WAS BLANK

move the "h" from "Ho" and put it in another word.

He said, "This is Westward 'O, a most hinteresting spot."

"It's where Kipling's story, 'Stalky and Co.,' took place," said Bob. "Tom told me to read it some time."

And while the Bentley's swift motor car bore them nearer and nearer to Clovelly, little Tom, far behind, trudged along on his own sturdy legs.

Evening fell and Tom stopped at a farmhouse. He explained that he was on his way home after a year's visit to America, and the simple farmers took him in.

He was so tired that, after tea, he fell into bed and asleep at almost the same moment.

CLOVELLY

Next morning he was up early. Then, with a hearty English breakfast tucked safely away, he thanked his hosts, and was off once more.

That afternoon Tom Jenks stood on the top of a hill, looking down at his native village.

Never, perhaps, has there been such a strangely adorable place as Clovelly. It is made of one narrow, cobbled street, steep as a mountain side, and it leads down to a tiny harbor.

Funny, crooked houses lean together, their peaked roofs whispering to one another. Not an automobile, not a wagon is allowed within Clovelly's walls. But little donkeys clatter busily up and down with loads on their backs.

Did you ever read in books about enchanted hamlets set far away beyond magic forests?

If you did, then you have imagined

Courtesy Associated British Railways, Inc.

CLOVELLY

Clovelly. But not quite! No description could prepare you for what you would see if you looked down upon it, as Tom now did.

Only, of course, your heart would not throb like the beat of a drum, because you had not been born there. But Tom Jenks had. So he must stand and rub a little tear out of his eye before he starts to climb down toward the house where he once lived.

He walked up to the door, knocked and took off his cap. A strange woman answered his knock. Where was his mother? His baby brother? Where were his two older sisters?

"They've moved away this past month," said the strange woman.

Tom stood like a little statue. He clutched his cap in stiff fingers and stared up at the woman with a frightened look on his face.

"Moved away?" he whispered. "Where— where have they gone?"

"I don't know, I'm sure," answered the woman. Then she added, as if sorry that she had spoken so shortly, "And who are you?"

"I—I'm Tom Jenks," the poor boy replied. His lip began to quiver. "I—I've come home from America, you know."

"Now, fancy!" gaped the woman. "And only yesterday there was an American lady

"WHERE HAVE THEY GONE?"

here asking for Tom Jenks. A grand-looking lady she was, too, with a lad about your own age."

Tom stared up at her but did not speak. How could he care about Bob Bentley's mother now, when his heart was so busy wanting his own mother?

"But," went on the woman indignantly, "I told them that this was not the home of the Jenks family. And so it isn't, for it belongs to me now!"

CHAPTER VI

THE JOURNEY

Tom found an old friend. He was a bewhiskered fisherman, who was very glad to
see Tom and took him inside his cozy cottage. Mrs. Fisherman, whose face was not
bewhiskered, but just as jolly and kind, gave
Tom a cup of tea.

The scent of flowers, the tinkling sound of
donkeys' hoofs on the cobblestones outside
brought to Tom memories of past happy
days in Clovelly. The fisherman told him all
he knew about the Jenks family.

"I dare say your mother is now in the town
of Stratford on Avon," he informed Tom.
"You'll remember she had a friend there
who worked at the Shakespeare Theatre?"

"Rather!" cried Tom. "It was Mrs. Butter, and she had charge of all the costumes

66

CLOVELLY

for the actors! Oh, I remember her well!"

"Well," continued the fisherman, "I expect it was this same Mistress Butter who sent for your mother to come and sew at the great Shakespeare Theatre. For you'll agree, my boy, that your mother is a clever one with the needle!"

Tom smiled for the first time. "Oh, rather!" he said. Then he jumped up from his chair and upset his tea. "Oh, I say!" he cried, "I must go to Stratford at once!"

The fisherman's wife caught him by the arm and drew him down into the chair again.

"You'll do nothing of the sort," she said. "You'll stop the night with us, young man, and tomorrow morning we shall set you off to Stratford, well rested and fed."

So Tom spent a night in Clovelly, and next morning, stuffed with food by the fisherman's good wife, he was ready to leave.

"Here is a bit of money for you," said the fisherman. He handed Tom some coins. "It's a long way to walk to Stratford."

But Tom had his wages as ship's page, so he thanked the fisherman and said that he would get along all right.

"No matter," insisted the old man. "Take these coins, laddie, and bring your wages to your mother, for I shouldn't wonder she'll be needing them."

Tom could not refuse his kind friend, so

he took the money and started to stuff it into his trousers pocket. But he felt the great hole there and remembered that he must keep his belongings in the other pocket until that hole was mended.

"Good-bye," he said to the two old people, "and I do thank you most awfully!"

"Good-bye, laddie!" sang out the Clovelly folk, as Tom began to climb up the quaint, cobbled street.

And that is how poor little Tom Jenks set out for Stratford, while Bob Bentley and his mother were also on their way to the town where William Shakespeare was born.

The Americans had been visiting many spots of interest, stopping whenever they felt so inclined. Mrs. Bentley spoke very little about Tom and the locket. Bob spoke even less. But both were busy with their thoughts.

Mrs. Bentley could not help thinking that Tom had lied to Bob about the location of his

home. She felt almost certain that the little
scamp had run off with her locket and that
she would never see it again.

Bob had told her that he had given Tom
their London address. So she wrote at once
to the hotel where they intended to stop, and
inquired whether a package had been received there for her.

She was in hopes that Tom might have
sent the locket to her when he discovered it,
though she doubted that he had.

But poor Bob hoped and prayed that his
friend would not disappoint him. What an
honest fellow Tom had appeared! And yet!
Now Bob suddenly remembered a remark
that Tom had made when he had gazed long-
ingly at the locket. He had said:

"Wouldn't my mother just love to have
such a locket! I do wish I might bring her
one!"

Oh, but he couldn't really believe that Tom
would steal!

"How far is it to the town of Bath, Mother?" asked Bob.

"Not very far," Mrs. Bentley replied. "Why do you want to know?"

"Because," Bob explained, "I've figured that the letter from our London hotel should be waiting for us at Bath."

Mrs. Bentley smiled. Her smile seemed to say, "Yes, the letter will no doubt be there, but it will tell us that the locket was not returned."

However, she did not speak these thoughts to Bob. Instead she took his hand and said:

"I'm sorry, son. It is a pity that your friend had to disappoint you; and after all he did in helping you to enjoy your books and your trip."

Bob could not speak. His voice was lost in a very full throat. Mrs. Bentley went on talking:

"I had hoped," she said, "that we might be able to help the poor little chap. Any boy who is so fond of learning deserves an education. So I was going to—"

"Oh, Moms!" broke in Bob. "Please don't blame Tom! I know he'll mail the locket back to us when he finds it! I know he will!"

But how could poor Tom send back something that he was not even aware he possessed? For, of course, the precious locket still lay at the bottom of his trouser leg!

And, speaking of Tom's trousers, they were beginning to make him feel most uncomfortable. People stared, for, in England, boys do not wear long, thick trousers, especially such odd, sailor-made trousers!

Once, as he walked through a village, a group of schoolboys shouted at him. Though they were older than he was, they wore short, grey breeches.

"Oh, I say!" yelled one. "Do have a look at the blighter in his father's clothes!"

"More likely his grandfather's!" shrieked another, and all screamed with laughter.

SHELLEY'S COTTAGE, LYNMOUTH

Tom hesitated, doubled up his fists, but decided not to stop. He must simply ignore these outbursts, else he would be fighting away his time and would never reach Stratford and his family.

However, Tom made up his mind to throw

LYNTON

away these trousers and secure a proper pair
of boys' breeches as soon as possible.

His route led him through the town of
Barnstaple, a port used by sailors in ancient
times. There is an old exchange here with
a curious stone tablet called the Nail.

Did you ever hear the expression, "paying on the nail"? It means to pay down, and it started long ago at this old exchange.

Tom was fortunate that day. A man driving one of those tiny British cars picked him up and saved him many weary steps.

By evening he was in the district of Lynton and Lynmouth. These are twin resorts, and the country round about is like a bit of Switzerland.

Tom walked up to the door of a little thatched cottage, set near a fern-banked glen. Tom never felt timid about asking for what he wanted. His smile and ruddy English face made him friends wherever he went.

He was met at the door by a forbidding woman, who looked a great deal like a horse. With her was a boy of about Tom's age.

"Good evening, madam," smiled Tom.

The woman glared at him crossly. She was the type of grown-up who seems to regard a boy simply as a noise with dirt sprinkled on it!

"May I have a bit of supper and a bed for the night?" asked Tom. "I'm quite able to pay, madam."

His dimple and the magic word, "pay," softened the woman's face and she took him in.

Next morning, as he was about to leave, the woman's nephew, Peter, came up to him. Peter was a timid country lad. He had a great admiration for Tom who, though his own age, was travelling all alone, dressed like a man.

"I say," he ventured, "you do look a bit of a toff in those long trousers!"

"I'd sooner be wearing your short ones!" returned Tom.

Then an idea came to him. Why not ask the boy to exchange trousers with him?

"Should you care to swap with me?" inquired Tom.

Peter's eyes gleamed. "Oh, rather!" he breathed.

So they took off their trousers, the little country lad thrilling with the prospect of wearing the clothes of a man. No doubt, city boys dressed like this in London town, though, of course, young Peter had never been there to see!

Tom sighed with relief as he stepped out of his long, clumsy trousers. At last people would not stare and shout at him on the streets! At last he would again look like a real English boy!

CHAPTER VII

THE LETTER

The Bentleys' car stopped at Stonehenge. This is England's finest ancient monument. Bob tried to remember all that Tom had told him about these mysterious stones. Rocky ruins, standing like waiting monsters of a past age. What had they once been?

Perhaps a temple for that ancient race, the Druids? Or a shrine built by the sun-worshippers? No one rightly knows the why of their beginning.

That night the Bentleys stopped at Winchester, which was once England's capital. There they saw the cathedral. It is the longest building in the world.

The following day they visited Glastonbury, where King Arthur lies buried. Here, also, is the Abbey which is the site of the

78

first Christian church erected in England.

A curious legend tells that the founder of this Abbey struck his staff into the ground and it grew into a tree. It became the Holy Thorn of Glastonbury and always blossomed on Christmas Day.

Many pilgrimages were made to this tree during the Middle Ages, and descendants of the Christmas-blooming plant still grow hereabouts.

As they drove along, Mrs. Bentley remarked upon the vivid coloring which she saw every place.

"Look!" she cried. "There is a picture!"

She pointed to a red-headed child, picking purple blossoms in a field near by.

The child wore a green dress trimmed with white. The blue sky and gold-green trees added two more colors; and, as if that were not enough, some pink-tinted sheep grazed not far off.

On the roads were many bicycle riders.

STONEHENGE

The women and girls wore khaki bloomers, their faces, arms and legs quite red from the sun.

Holidays spell picnics to most British folk. And there are many holidays on this brisk little island. So groups of roadside merrymakers can usually be found, enjoying their beloved fresh air and exercise.

"Nearly all the houses are built of stone or brick," said Bob. "I wonder why."

Harkness, the chauffeur, replied:

"That is because there is very little wood in England, Master Robert. The country is so old, you know, that almost all the trees have been chopped down. Therefore, wood is frightfully valuable."

Bob had found that Harkness usually had intelligent answers to his questions. In fact, it amazed Bob to hear how everyone they addressed, even ragged urchins on the streets, were well-spoken and intelligent.

Bob also noticed how motorists tried to make it easy for other drivers along the highway. They would cheerfully wave you on if you chanced to be in back of their cars and wanted to pass.

They would smile at you or warn you if something were coming; but Bob saw no

ROMAN BATHS, BATH

scowling faces behind steering wheels.

At last they reached the town of Bath where they decided to remain a day or so. Mrs. Bentley wanted to try the famous healing waters.

PUMP ROOM, BATH

Bob could hardly wait to arrive at their hotel where they expected to find that letter from London. Had Tom returned the locket? The letter would tell.

But Harkness insisted upon driving them around Bath and telling them proudly that it was founded by the Romans in the first century. Harkness spoke as though he had been with the Romans at the time, assisting with everything!

Bob glanced about absent-mindedly.

"Oh, yes, yes," he agreed with Harkness. It was a "most extraordinary city!" Yes, yes, the streets were unusually wide and beautiful!

Oh, yes, indeed, it was "jolly interesting" that the Romans had called the city Aquae Solis (Waters of the Sun) and built handsome baths, which were later dug up!

But Bob's thoughts were elsewhere. They were with a letter which should have arrived from London.

At last Harkness tore himself away from the ancient Romans and drove the Americans to their hotel. There the letter was indeed awaiting them!

Mrs. Bentley read it to Bob. Of course, the London hotel had received no package for the Bentleys!

Bob's heart sank as he watched the look of disappointment come over his mother's face. He knew well what she must be thinking about the little page, and he could not blame her!

He began to feel the same way about Tom Jenks. Horrid little beast! Pretending to be his friend and then stealing from him! For, of course, Tom must have known, when he found the locket, that it was not meant for him!

After their stay in Bath, they continued on toward Stratford on Avon.

Their route took them through Gloucester, where they gazed upon the New Inn, a building which is only five centuries old! They also saw the magnificent cathedral and the Deanery, said to be the oldest inhabited house in Britain.

THE FIVE CENTURY OLD "NEW INN," GLOUCESTER

Of course Tom was impressed with the age
and stateliness of all these ancient places.
But other things, more modern, also cap-

tured his interest and made him curious.

For instance, he remarked that there were cats everywhere!   In shops, in restaurants, in windows, on the streets!   Friendly beasts, they rubbed up against one and spoke in soft British purrs!

The old nursery rhyme came to Bob's mind:

> "Pussycat, pussycat,
> Where have you been?
> I've been to London
> To visit the Queen."

Did the creatures even go to visit the Queen?

Then, there was the well-known story of Dick Whittington and his cat, which Tom had said he liked so much!

Where was Tom now—the rascal?

The "rascal" happened to be in difficulty!

CHAPTER VIII

THE DISAPPOINTMENT

The "rascal" was taking off his trousers! So was the country lad, whose name was Peter. They were trading, or, as they called it, swapping.

Suddenly young Peter gave a gasp. "My word, the dragon's coming!" he gulped.

"What do you mean?" asked Tom, thrusting one foot through the leg of the other boy's short breeches.

"My aunt," breathed Peter, "and she'll raise an awful row when she sees what we're doing! Oh, I say, you'd better hurry and bolt!" As he spoke, he pulled on Tom's long trousers.

Now Tom had no desire to meet Peter's horse-faced aunt in a temper. She was unpleasant enough out of one!

88

"Right-o!" answered Tom. "I'll be going!"

He started hastily out the door but found walking a bit difficult. The reason for this was that he had put on Peter's breeches back to front!

So, making little leaps, he dashed out and across the lawn, looking for all the world like a stout jack rabbit.

Aunt "Dragon," however, must have belonged to the race-horse family, for soon Tom found himself held firmly by the ear.

"So!" gabbled the furious woman. "You thought you could get away from me, did you? What do you mean by trying to steal my nephew's breeches?"

Tom breathed hard. "I didn't try to steal them!" he panted. "I gave him my trousers in exchange!"

Peter's aunt sniffed. "I shouldn't wonder!" she replied. "And a nice-looking pair of trousers *they* are, to be sure! Return to

the house at once and give back my
nephew's new breeches! Look sharp now!"

Tom returned to the house, assisted by
little punches from Peter's aunt, and there
he and the country lad made another exchange.

So that was how Tom Jenks started out
again for Stratford, wearing his old trousers
with Mrs. Bentley's locket lying at the bottom of one leg!

Bob and his mother were also drawing
closer to Stratford. But while poor little
Tom Jenks was seriously searching for his
family, fortunate Bob Bentley was in quest
only of amusement.

"May we go to the Shakespeare Theatre
tonight, Mother?" asked the American boy.

"Yes, dear," said Mrs. Bentley, "and I
hope it will be a play that you'll enjoy."

Harkness grinned mysteriously and
stopped the car at a town called Evesham,
where Market Day was in full swing. It was

an old-fashioned town in the center of a fer-
tile orchard land.

The chauffeur went into a shop and came
out again, beaming like an automobile head
lamp!

He started the car, then turned to Bob
and said, "I've jolly news for you, Master
Robert!"

"What is it, Harkness?" asked Bob.

"It's 'The Taming of the Shrew' at the
Shakespeare Theatre tonight," he announced. "That is one of the funniest
comedies of all!   Isn't that ripping?"

"What's ripping?   My coat?" asked Bob,
startled.

Harkness turned a ripe tomato color while
Mrs. Bentley explained:

"The English use the word 'ripping' as we
use 'fine' or 'great.'

Bob scratched his head. Heavens! Did
he or did he not speak the English language? He guessed he did not!

Courtesy Topical Press Agency

SHAKESPEARE'S BIRTHPLACE, STRATFORD ON AVON

That evening they arrived at Stratford in time for dinner. Bob was delighted with the quaint Shakespeare Inn, where they stopped.

The old hall smelled of mopped floors and cold mutton. As they passed the kitchen, Bob peeked in and saw big, bright copper kettles hanging on the walls. Little, frightened serving maids dodged here and there.

Mrs. Bentley secured theatre tickets from the hall porter. He was an aproned individual, worried-eyed and all-important. He informed them that the play was not to be "The Taming of the Shrew" after all, but "Othello," one of Shakespeare's famous tragedies.

Each room at the inn was marked with the title of a play by Shakespeare. The Bentleys were shown to "All's Well That Ends Well."

"I wish it would!" sighed Bob to himself. He was thinking of his lost friend, Tom— Tom, who had done so much to help him to enjoy this trip, and then had done something else to spoil it for him!

That night they attended the Shakespeare Memorial Theatre, a very modern building, simple and charming in its design.

"The stage has no footlights, Mother," whispered Bob, as the curtain went up.

"No," replied Mrs. Bentley, "but the lighting effects are quite beautiful in spite of that."

While the play was going on, someone arrived at the stage door, asking eagerly to see a Mrs. Jenks.

This someone was a rather plump little boy, with rumpled, blond hair, wearing long, shabby trousers.

"She's my mother, if you please, sir," he said. "And I dare say she'll be in the costume department."

"We've no Mrs. Jenks here, my boy," the doorman said. "However," he added, "we've a Mrs. Butter, who's in charge of the

THE SHAKESPEARE THEATRE, STRATFORD ON AVON

costumes. Should you care to talk to her?"
Tom, swallowing hard, said that he should
and the doorman called Mrs. Butter. Pres-
ently an enlarged butter-ball came waddling
out of somewhere. She matched her name,
did Mrs. Butter. She was quite round and

her plump face glistened with good nature.

"Why, Tommy Jenks!" she gurgled happily. "You precious little nipper! Wherever do you come from?"

She folded Tom in a sea of black dress and nearly smothered him. Tom wriggled loose and she put her finger to his mouth.

"Sh!" she cautioned. "Not another word!" (Tom had not spoken once!) "Come to my sewing room where we shall be alone and not disturb the actors upon the stage! Come, darling!"

When they were in the wardrobe chamber where Mrs. Butter worked, Tom at last found an opportunity to ask for his mother.

"They told me in Clovelly," said the boy, "that I should find her here. Where is she, please?"

"She's in London!" answered stout Mrs. Butter, and her face fell as if it had been melted in a hot pan. "Poor lambie!"

Tom's lip began to tremble. His blue eyes

began to fill. He was so tired, so homesick!
And, after this long trip, his family was not
here at all!

"She was offered a position in London, you
see," said Mrs. Butter. "The work is at a
big hotel, mark you! Oh, I'm frightfully
pleased about it as it pays quite good wages.

"Still, Tommy, your family is obliged to
make quite a struggle, as it's no holiday pic-
nic for a woman left alone! Ah, 'twas a pity
your good father had to go—

"Oh, come now!" she broke off and drew
the sobbing little boy close to her. "Hush,
my dearie," she soothed. "Do stop crying;
there's a good lad! See! We'll go to my
lodgings and have a perfectly enormous
supper! How would you like that?"

Her eyes shone as she rocked Tom back
and forth. Anyone could see that the idea
of an enormous supper appealed to her
strongly.

CHAPTER IX

THE HOME OF SHAKESPEARE

Bob Bentley did not know that Tom Jenks was in Stratford. And, of course, Tom did not know that Bob was also there.

Next morning Tom awoke in Mrs. Butter's bed and sniffed a delicious odor. Mrs. Butter was already busy in the kitchen, and Tom could hear her humming away to the tune of sizzling sausages.

Tom felt much better. After all, London was not very far away. He could be there this evening if someone would again stop and give him a ride in an automobile.

He stretched and sighed comfortably, turned over on his side, and started to drop off to sleep again. But no! He must get up and see a bit of Stratford before leaving the birthplace of his favorite poet.

He hopped out of bed. Where were his trousers? He called to Mrs. Butter and she appeared in the doorway.

"Bless you, dearie!" she beamed, looking, in her kitchen apron, like a well-filled circus tent. "I've your trousers, and I'll fetch them for you directly. There was such a great hole in the pocket that I just had to sew it up."

She brought the trousers to Tom and he dressed. Then, feeling like a starved bear cub, he sat down to breakfast with her.

Now, that same morning Bob Bentley and his mother decided to go sight-seeing in the famous town. They wandered about for a while on the banks of the River Avon.

Small boys, their legs dangling from the wall, were busily fishing. Boats, with singing holiday-makers, glided on the shining water. It was on these very shores that the young Shakespeare had played and dreamed.

Bob and his mother strolled through the twisting streets of Stratford. Bob kept

Courtesy Associated British Railways, Inc.
SHOTTERY VILLAGE, NEAR STRATFORD

thinking of "Othello," the play that he had
seen last night. What a dreadful amount of
villainy and stabbing there was in it!

Mrs. Bentley broke in upon his thoughts. "Here is the old school where Will Shakespeare studied," she said. "When he was a boy, school lasted for twelve hours a day."

"No wonder he wrote 'Othello' when he grew up!" said Bob, with feeling.

They saw the American Fountain, built by American tourists; also the Harvard House, which had once belonged to the parents of John Harvard, who helped to found Harvard University.

Inside the house where Shakespeare was born, the Bentleys listened to a lecture by a guide. He recited facts about the poet which Bob already knew. Tom Jenks had told him all those things! Where was Tom now?

Tom Jenks was standing right outside the gate of Shakespeare's house at that very moment!

He wanted very much to go inside, but he did not dare spend a shilling out of his precious money. He knew that his mother would be able to make very good use of it.

But, oh, he would so like to see the room where his idol had once lived! Yes, he must go in!

He fingered his money and started up the walk to the door. Then, once again, he thought of his poor mother, working so hard to support her large family! Sewing all day long in the linen room of a London hotel!

A shilling might buy food for a whole meal! No, he would not go in!

But what an opportunity really to see something that he had read about all his life! Oh, he *would* go in!

"See here, Tom Jenks," he scolded himself, "you'll jolly well come right along now! You shall go and bid good-bye to Mrs. Butter and be off for London at once!"

So saying, Tom turned on his heel and made swiftly for Mrs. Butter's lodgings, leaving Shakespeare and Bob Bentley behind.

CHAPTER X

THE HOME OF TOM JENKS

It is said that nearly every Englishman goes to London some time in his life. And why not? It takes but a day to reach the world's largest city from anywhere on the small island.

So Tom arrived the next afternoon. He had travelled most of the way on the side seat of a "motor-bike," or motorcycle.

Tom found London wrapped in a burning heat. It struck him as unnatural, for all his life he had heard of chill London fogs.

But it was summer time now. The parks were overflowing with sizzling children, trying to cool themselves in the lakes. Some wore only thin bloomers, while others scampered about in nothing but happy smiles.

He thrilled to be walking the streets of

Courtesy Photochrom Co., Ltd.
ST. PAUL'S CATHEDRAL, LONDON

London, which he had known only between the covers of books. No other city is so full of great men and women and events.

Somehow, London smelled horsy. Yes,

comfortable and old-world and horsy! Just
as if she had said to herself:

"I am the largest city in the world. Modern, too, with my fine shops, crowded streets,
and motor cars! Yet why should I rush
madly about, screech until I am hoarse, and
perfume myself with smoke and petrol?

"No, I'll just leave all that to my young
and madcap sister, New York, with her
ridiculous, many-storied hats! I prefer to
dress in my ancient, solid buildings, keep
alive my history, and continue to smell a bit
horsy!"

Tom went directly to the hotel where Mrs.
Butter had told him that his mother worked.
He was shown to the linen room, not daring
to believe that, at last, he was really going
to find her!

He paused on the threshold of the door
and looked in. Yes, there she was, the same
kind-faced mother whom he had not seen
for over a year.

Mrs. Jenks was carrying in her arms a huge pile of sheets. When she saw her son standing in the doorway, she gave a little cry and dropped the sheets—bung!

"Tommy! Lord bless my soul!" she gasped. Then she rushed toward him.

Tom made a manful effort to smile and toss off a "Oh, hello, Mother! I say, but I'm jolly glad to see you—" or something of the sort. But do you think he did that? He did not!

"M-m-mother!" was all he could manage. The rest was a jumble of tears and sobs, as, with a heart full of relief and joy, he threw himself into her arms.

He stayed with his mother until her work was done. Then she took him home with her.

The Jenks family lived in a poor, tiny flat on one of London's dingy streets. Tom was met by his two sisters and his little brother.

The oldest, Alice, beamed with delight

Courtesy Associated British Railways, Inc.

HORSE GUARDS PASSING THE GUARDS MEMORIAL

when she saw him and cried, "Oh, Tom! Fancy having you home with us again!"

The second sister, Martha, caught him by the coat and spun him around like a top, screaming, "What luck! Oh, I say, what luck, Tom!"

Little David, the youngest, leaped upon Tom like a frenzied puppy and squealed, "Tommy! Tommy! Tommy!"

In fact, the family gave Tom such a hearty welcome that he felt like the King receiving the keys to the city!   He was reminded of an old ceremony which still takes place in London every year.

The Lord Mayor once ruled over the ancient city, while Westminster was the King's domain.   Temple Bar in Fleet Street was the boundary line between the two sections.

If the Lord Mayor so desired, he could refuse the King admittance to the city.

Every year the King and his followers arrived at the Temple Bar and asked to be allowed in.   The Mayor always opened the gates, presenting the ruler with keys to the city and a jeweled sword.

The Jenks family gave their young "king" fish paste and an egg for his tea that evening.

Tom, feeling quite a man, announced that he would help support the family.

Mrs. Jenks felt a wave of sadness sweep

over her, because, to her, Tommy still looked
a very little boy.

But she knew how badly the family needed
his help, so she said, "I shouldn't wonder if
the manager of the hotel where I work could
use another page boy."

Therefore, next day, Tom again accom-
panied his mother when she went to work.

The hotel manager liked Tom's smile and
found him intelligent. He engaged him as
a page and told him to report for duty on the
following day.

They gave him a uniform which, however,
was too large. So, that evening, when
Mrs. Jenks arrived home, she proceeded to
cut it to fit her son.

Little David cast longing looks at Tom's
old trousers. "I say, Tom," he ventured.
"Will you give them to me now that you are
to have such a beautiful new uniform?"

Tom laughed at his roly-poly little brother
and rumpled his curly hair. "They'll be

WINDSOR CASTLE AND THE THAMES RIVER

frightfully large for you, Davie," he said. "But, as you're a rum little toad, I expect I'll let you have them!"

David caught up the trousers and ran to his older sister, waving them around like a flag.

"Oh, Alice! Alice!" he cried. "See what brother has given me! Do cut them to fit

me, at once! Mother is busy sewing on
Tommy's uniform."

So Alice, who was eighteen and a good
sewer like her mother, took the trousers and
sat down beside the lamp.

"I shall have to cut them off at the knee,
Davie," she said. "You're too young for
long trousers, you know."

Alice picked up her scissors and studied
the trousers. (Oh, little locket down there
in the left leg, has the time come for you to
be discovered?)

But Alice wrinkled up her nose in disgust.
What disgraceful-looking trousers they
were! How she should like to throw them
away and buy Davie a new pair of breeches!

Alice sighed. Oh, well, people must make
the best of things when they were poor! So
she started to cut, when suddenly the door-
bell rang.

Alice arose, leaving the trousers on the
chair.

"I expect it's Alice's bobby!" teased Martha.

English policemen are called bobbies. And it was indeed Alice's bobby, an apple-cheeked young man, who insisted upon taking Alice to the London Museum.

This is an enchanting place where one can see all manner of historical models. There is one of old London Bridge, which recalls the rhyme, "London Bridge is falling down."

There is a model of London's great fire of the year 1666. It shows the burning of the city, by means of clever lighting.

It seemed to Alice that every time she visited the London Museum she found new wonders at which to marvel.

She now went to her room to put on her hat and coat, calling to the waiting bobby that she'd be there directly. When she returned, ready to go, she saw that little Davie's face was screwed up like a baked apple!

"Oh, darling," cried Alice, throwing her arms about her little brother, "don't cry! I'll cut the trousers for you tomorrow! Truly I shall!"

But Davie's looks were still black. He had planned to show himself off to the neighborhood tomorrow in his big brother's clothes, and he was disappointed.

"Good night, all!" sang Alice, and the door shut behind her.

So Tom's old trousers lay neglected on the chair. And little David went to bed, disliking the London Museum and all apple-cheeked bobbies who took girls to see it.

Aid

checked

CHAPTER XI

THE BENTLEYS' TOUR

Back to Bob Bentley and his mother.

The American tourists had stopped another day in Stratford in order to visit the
surrounding points of interest.

First, there was Warwick, a fairy tale
castle with a fairy tale hero, whose name
was Guy of Warwick. He was supposed to
be a giant and his huge suit of armor can
still be seen in the hall of the castle.

But the sedate old place, set in its beautiful gardens, was really the home of Alfreda,
daughter of King Alfred the Great.

The name of Richard Neville, one of the
earls of Warwick, recalls the War of the
Roses. It was fought in the fifteenth century between the families of York and Lancaster.

KENILWORTH CASTLE

The badge of Lancaster was a red rose; the badge of York, a white rose. Both houses claimed the English throne, and so powerful was Richard Neville during this time that he has been called "The King Maker."

Next came Kenilworth Castle, one of the most fascinating ruined castles in existence.

Bob had read Sir Walter Scott's "Kenilworth," which tells of royal festivities in the days of Queen Elizabeth.

Sheep now peacefully nibble grass where once trod the great Earl of Leicester and his princely guests. The castle is now a stable.

Bob gazed up at broken windows which, at one time, framed the graceful heads of princesses. At one of these windows, two woolly tails stuck out, and Bob laughed.

They passed through Rugby, the famous boys' school. It was here that the game of Rugby football was born, and from it came our own American football.

Then on they went to Sulgrave. Here the ancestors of George Washington had lived. Today the dignified house is a museum.

Bob suddenly stopped, with his eyes raised, and whispered to his mother, "Look, Moms! It's Old Glory!"

SULGRAVE MANOR

And, sure enough, the American flag was
flying beside the house. It did something to
the spine of an American boy to watch the
stars and stripes flutter in a British breeze!

Bob remembered what Tom had said the
day they had fought on board ship.

"England and America have the same history and heroes," he had reminded Bob.

"England is home to most Americans, because your ancestors set out from there to discover your country!"

Tom had been such a friendly boy! So entertaining! A good pal! Why didn't he send back that locket?

> "Ride a cockhorse
> To Banbury Cross—"

The Bentleys were driving through the rather bleak town of Banbury. Bob looked long at the famous Banbury Cross.

"Where is the hobbyhorse?" he asked Harkness.

"Oh, there's no such thing, you know, Master Robert," the chauffeur replied. "Nobody rightly knows where the old rhyme started. They do say, however, that it goes back to the May Day celebration when the May Queen rode through town on a white horse."

Bob wanted to try some Banbury cakes

MAY DAY CELEBRATION, BANBURY CROSS

as they, like the rhyme, have an ancient history. It seems that, on May Day, years ago, the children rolled these cakes down a hill, and woe to the child whose cake broke in the rolling. Great trouble was supposed to come to him.

We often hear the expression, "Stupid as an ox," and it happened that Bob and his mother were now approaching a place which was named after oxen. Yet the strange part is that here is one of the world's important schools of learning!

Oxford is England's oldest university. At one time the oxen used to cross, or "ford," the River Thames, so the place was called "Oxen-ford." And that is how the home of scholars came to be named after dull beasts!

The Bentleys wandered about, and Bob found that the university is composed of twenty-seven colleges.

One of the most beautiful colleges is Magdalen, with its cloisters, lovely archways, and flower gardens. Bob was amazed to hear the name pronounced "Maudlen"!

New College is among the oldest, and Queen's College is where many great men have studied. Christ Church College is also full of historic memories.

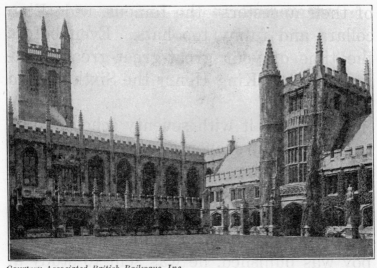

Courtesy Associated British Railways, Inc.

THE CLOISTERS, MAGDALEN COLLEGE, OXFORD

In fact, Bob felt as if he had walked into the past, surrounded by the dignity and solid grandeur of old Oxford.

But possibly Bob enjoyed even more their visit to Eton, the well-known school for younger boys. Sons of kings, men of renown have studied here in Eton's somber, ivy-covered buildings.

See those little lads wearing the costumes

of their ancestors—the famous, wide Eton
collars and funny top hats. Even before
the time of your great-great-great-great-
grandfather, King Henry the Sixth started
Eton.

He started it with seventy scholars, and
today there are over one thousand. But
only seventy boys may live in the school and
they are called "King's scholars."

Strange old customs are handed down
from ancient times. For instance, when a
boy was punished, he was sent to study at
the back of the schoolroom where there were
no candles.

The room was without windows, so in bad
weather the shutters were drawn. Poor
little dunce! He must work alone in the
dark!

For this reason the front part of the school
room became known as "Sense," while the
dark, rear part was called "Nonsense"!

Bob left Eton with mixed feelings. He

ETON SCHOLARS

could not quite imagine what it would be like to arise early and study until six o'clock, tea time. Then to bed early, too, so as to be up for morning chapel.

No motion pictures. Not much fun. Nevertheless, there was something about it all which fascinated the American boy.

Near by Eton stands Windsor Castle, one of the residences of the King and Queen.

At the time the royal family was living at Buckingham Palace in London, so visitors were permitted to go inside.

A curious crowd pushed its way through the castle, and, though it was magnificent, Bob somehow was glad he was not a king!

"The curfew tolls the knell of parting day;
The lowing herd winds slowly o'er the lea;
The plowman homeward plods his weary
    way
And leaves the world to darkness and
    to me."

Harkness suddenly began to recite the above lines, through his nose. Bob looked at him anxiously and wondered what had come over him.

"Don't you know what that is, Master Robert?" inquired the chauffeur.

Bob did not know.

GRAY'S CHURCH, STOKE POGES

"Oh!" Harkness seemed astonished. "It is, I dare say, the best known poem in the English language!" he declared. "It is Thomas Gray's 'Elegy in a Country Churchyard,' and here we are now at the churchyard itself!"

There were the little village church of
Stoke Poges, the poet's tomb, and the peace-
ful, old-fashioned graveyard. Bob decided
to read this beautiful poem as soon as possible.

They arrived at Hampton Court, a palace
built by Cardinal Wolsey and also occupied
by many kings and queens. In the exquisite
garden is a maze where children play.

Screams could be heard a long way off, because once you enter this hedged-in place of
mystery, it is almost impossible to get out
again.

"It looks easy!" sniffed Bob, and in he
sauntered, with his nose in the air.

He walked and walked and turned and
twisted along the confusing paths. Then he
walked some more, and then he turned and
twisted some more, trying to get out. But
he was still imprisoned in the maze!

"Turn to your right next corner!" shouted
a freckled girl.

Bob did as she told him and bumped straight into a high hedge!

"Ouch!" he cried, rubbing his nose.

He could hear a howl of joy from the freckled girl and her companions. It made him furious.

So let us leave Bob here, more lost and more angry every minute, while we return to London and Tom Jenks.

(Yes, Bob will find his way out of the maze. Everyone always does!)

CHAPTER XII

THE DISCOVERY

Tom returned home that evening, delighted with his new job. He had liked run-
ning errands for tourists who came from all
parts of the world. He had been much
pleased with the generous tips he had received from the gentlemen, and the kind
smiles given him by the ladies.

He looked smaller than ever in his tight-
fitting page's uniform with the brass buttons. So, naturally, the hotel guests had
tried to spoil him.

At supper the family listened eagerly to
his glowing tales. After supper, Tom, tired
from his day's work, went straight to bed.

Mrs. Jenks had brought home some sewing and busied herself with it. The younger
sister, Martha, sat on the floor with little

David and amused him by coloring a picture book.

Older sister Alice sat down beside the lamp and took up Tom's trousers. She had promised Davie that she would cut them to fit him and he would give her no peace until she did it.

But it seemed a pity to waste time on such a shabby-looking garment! Perhaps now that Tommy had a job, they could afford to buy Davie a pair of new breeches and throw these dreadful things away!

David broke in upon Alice's thoughts. "Do start cutting the trousers for me, Alice!" he begged. "I shall want to wear them tomorrow!"

"Right-o, darling," she smiled.

"After all," she thought to herself, "Davie doesn't care how bad they look so long as they had belonged to his big brother!"

She began to cut.

After David and Martha had gone to bed,

LITTLE TOM IN HIS UNIFORM

Alice looked at the results of her work. The old trousers made a fairly good-looking pair of breeches for Davie. He would be pleased.

The trouser legs which she had cut off lay on the floor. Alice now stooped to pick them up. She would put them away in the scrap bag.

She shook them out, and as she did so something fell out of one leg!

Alice stooped again, and could hardly believe her eyes! Why, here were two paper bills, each representing to Alice Jenks a vast amount of money! Oh, how could Tommy have been so careless?

But what was this thing that she now found nestled in one of the paper notes? A diamond locket! In the center was set the picture of some strange gentleman!

"Mother!" called Alice. "Do come here at once and see what I've found in the leg of Tommy's old trousers!"

Mrs. Jenks was just as puzzled as Alice over the discovery.

"Shall I wake Tom, Mother?" asked Alice.

Mrs. Jenks shook her head. "No," she replied. "The poor boy is tired. Let him sleep."

She took the money and the locket out of Alice's hand.

"I'll put them carefully away until morning," she said. "Then we shall ask Tommy to tell us all about it."

By this time the Bentleys had reached London and were now settled at their fashionable hotel. Mrs. Bentley had again inquired whether a package had been received for her and the answer, of course, was no.

Now that he was at last in London, Bob

Courtesy Associated British Railways, Inc.

TOWER OF LONDON

kept thinking more and more of Tom Jenks.

Sometimes his thoughts were black. But sometimes Bob could not help remembering the little page with pleasure and gratitude.

Especially was this true during his sight-seeing tour through London. How much more interesting was the Tower of London when Bob recalled everything that Tom had told him about it!

Those stories of tragedy connected with this gloomy, old fortress! The bloody Tower, where Sir Walter Raleigh was imprisoned, and where he wrote a history of the world.

A small stone room in this same tower brought back a dreadful memory. It was here that two young princes, Edward and Richard, were murdered by their uncle, the cruel Duke of Gloucester.

Tower Green is the spot where many unfortunates lost their heads, among them two of the wives of Henry the Eighth.

A collection of fierce-looking axes and other implements of death are displayed in the Tower. Indeed, it is a most horrible place, and therefore Bob, who was ten years old, enjoyed himself thoroughly.

Mrs. Bentley spent a long while admiring the crowns, scepters, and other glittering possessions of the royal family. They are displayed in a round, glass case.

Bob watched the changing of the guard at Buckingham Palace. From a distance, the stiff guards in their small sentry boxes stood like toy soldiers. They wore bright red coats and high, bearskin hats, called busbies.

When Bob approached the massive iron gates of the Palace, it seemed more like the domain of a giant. And, indeed, the King and Queen of England are beloved giants in the hearts of their loyal subjects.

Bob was also deeply impressed by the King's Horse Guards. Tall soldiers with plumes in their shining helmets rode forth in glory upon sleek, prancing horses.

"London is like a grand parade, isn't it, Mother?" said Bob, his eyes dancing with excitement.

"The English are fond of splendor and ceremony," answered Mrs. Bentley. "But they say that the King and Queen are as friendly and natural as they can be."

"I would like to see the Prince of Wales,"

said Bob, though what this title meant, he had no idea! He decided to ask his mother.

Mrs. Bentley laughed. "Haven't you ever heard of the little country of Wales?" she asked him. "It is in Great Britain. But long ago it was not a part of the kingdom and the people have always spoken a language of their own.

"At last, however, an English king conquered them. The story goes that he promised them a ruler who was born in Wales and who could not speak a word of English.

"This pleased the Welsh, for they expected it to be one of their own people. But, instead of this, the King arranged to have his baby son born in Wales. And, of course, the infant could not speak a word of English!

"So the King's son became the ruler of the Welsh and ever since then the King's first-born has been known as the Prince of Wales."

A GUARD IN A SENTRY BOX

Bob visited old Westminster Abbey. Here he saw carved figures of kings and queens, the shrine of the World War's Unknown Soldier, and the graves of England's greatest poets.

A guide pointed out the Coronation Chair, in which all of England's kings have been crowned since Edward the First.

Under the Coronation Chair is built the

Stone of Scone, where the Scotch kings used to be crowned. Now, however, England and Scotland are ruled by the British King, so His Majesty must sit upon both coronation chairs at once!

Crouching in the shadow of Westminster Abbey is the Westminster School, built by King Henry the Eighth.

Bob was amazed to see boys of his own age dressed in what appeared to be stage costumes. But he discovered that it was the garb of their ancestors.

He was even more astonished when he visited the Blue Coat School near St. James' Park. Here the boys were playing cricket, the national English game.

Bob rubbed his eyes to make sure that he was not dreaming, for these boys wore long, blue coats to their ankles, bright yellow stockings, and red leather belts!

Bob wrinkled up his nose and almost said, "Sissies!" Then he thought of Tom Jenks!

CHAPTER XIII

THE STREETS OF LONDON

Tom Jenks' sister, Alice, came into his room next morning holding out the locket and the money.

"I found them in the leg of your trousers, Tom," said Alice. "However did they—?"

But she got no further. Tom leaped out of bed and snatched the locket and the money out of her hand.

"I say! Oh—I say!" cried Tom, purple in the face. "They're Bob Bentley's! The locket's his mother's! She was most frightfully fond of it! However did it get into my trouser leg?"

"And these paper bills, Tom!" added Alice. "Where did they come from?"

"I'll jolly well find out!" Tom exclaimed, and he hopped about the room, dressing in record time.

WESTMINSTER ABBEY

Then he went in to breakfast with his hair standing up on end because he had been too excited to brush it down.

"I shall go round to Bob's hotel," he gulped, and promptly choked over his porridge.

His mother clapped him on the back to make him stop choking. When he could talk again, he continued.

"It was that beastly hole in my pocket," he said. "Bob Bentley must have put the money in my pocket and the locket fell in by mistake! I shall return both at once! It's a good job I know where the Bentleys are stopping! Whatever must they think of me?"

"But how do you know that your American friends are still in London, Tom?" asked Alice anxiously.

Tom dropped his knife and fork with a clatter. The kippered herring flew off his plate and hit David in the eye.

"Oh, I'd not thought of that!" breathed poor Tom. "I say, if they're no longer here, I shan't ever be able to return the locket, and Mrs. Bentley will think me a thief!"

Mrs. Jenks started to remove plates from the table.

"Now then, don't you worry, dearie," she said to Tom. "I dare say you'll find them at their hotel. Trippers always remain a long time in dear old London! There's so much for them to see, you know!"

Tom knew Bob Bentley's address, for Bob had given it to him on the boat. So he kissed his mother good-bye and, clutching the money and locket in his hand, he was off.

He shot through Piccadilly Circus, which is not a circus of performing elephants and brass bands but a wide, city square. Yet you might well be confused by the heavy traffic and crisscrossing streets, just as you are by three rings of acrobats and animals!

People stared at Tom as he rushed madly

Courtesy Associated British Railways, Inc.

THE GUARDS BAND PASSING BUCKINGHAM PALACE

along. He ran past dignified shops and buildings and they seemed to raise their weather-beaten, stone eyebrows at him and say, "Fancy!" Once he nearly crashed into a street bus, and a passenger sitting up on top did say, "Fancy!"

At last, puffing like a fox-hunting hound,

he reached Bob Bentley's hotel. He stumbled up the steps, making a little prayer to himself.

"Please let Bob be here, dear God! Please!" he prayed.

He faced a sour-looking clerk in a very high collar, who stood behind the desk.

"Beg pardon, sir," gasped Tom. "Is there a chap named Bentley here?"

The clerk, hardly noticing the eager, round face upturned to his, replied in a bored manner, "No, he's not here—"

Tom Jenks' heart threatened to stop beating.

"He and his mother have gone—" continued the clerk.

Then the telephone rang and he turned to answer it.

"Are you there?" he asked, which is what the English often say instead of "hello."

When the clerk had finished his telephone conversation, he again turned to Tom. His expression was blank, as if he had forgotten why the boy was there.

"Oh—" he remembered, "you were asking for Master Bentley!"

"Yes, sir!" said Tom.

"Oh, quite!" agreed the clerk. "Why, he and his mother have gone sight-seeing, you know. Anything I can do for you, boy?"

A weight fell suddenly from Tom's chest. Bob Bentley was still in London!

"Oh, no, thank you, sir!" he told the clerk. "I'll be round later—" And he was gone!

He would have to hurry back to his job. He was late.

But Tom had decided to return once again to the American boy's hotel when his own day's work was over. By that time he felt sure that Bob would be home from his sight-seeing tour.

Nobody, thought the little page, but he should return that locket and money to the Bentleys!

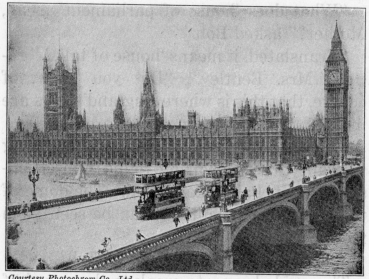

Courtesy Photochrom Co., Ltd.

HOUSES OF PARLIAMENT

He must try to make his friend Bob understand how it had all happened. For whatever was Bob thinking of him now?

Bob was not thinking of him at all! He was, at that moment, thinking about the Houses of Parliament! With his mother, Bob stood in Parliament Square, gazing up at the somber, grey buildings.

"What does 'house of parliament' mean, Mother?" asked Bob.

"Translated, it means 'house of talk,' " replied Mrs. Bentley. "But you know, of course, that this is where England's laws are made."

Later in the day, when Bob was beginning to want to sit down, he found himself inspecting St. Paul's Cathedral. The dome of this magnificent building can be seen from most parts of London.

Why did it look so familiar to Bob?

The guide began to croak to the crowd of tourists:

"They say that the dome of the Capitol in Washington, United States of America, was copied from this dome of St. Paul's."

Then Bob knew why it had seemed familiar.

They entered the cathedral and Mrs. Bentley told Bob that it was exquisite. Bob answered that his feet hurt!

They arrived at a circular gallery above the arches.

"This is the Whispering Gallery," said the guide. "It is so called because a whisper can be heard from one side to the other."

He turned to Bob. "Here, young man," he said. "You go over on the other side and whisper anything you care to."

Bob forgot about his feet. But once on the opposite side, he could think of nothing to say and was suddenly terrified.

"Whisper!" commanded the guide.

"Hello!" puffed Bob, feeling like an actor speaking his first part on the stage!

But the people across the cathedral heard him plainly.

Outside Harkness met them with the car, and Bob was glad to sink back on the cushions and rest. He was hoping that they would not do any more sight-seeing today, when Harkness, with a proud glitter in his eye, suggested a visit to Hyde Park.

But, once again, Bob forgot to be tired as he walked through Kensington Gardens and thought of Peter Pan. They saw the statue of Sir James Barrie's little boy who wouldn't grow up. It stands by the side of a stream where children sail boats.

English "nannies," nurses in bonnets and long capes, were pushing their baby prams home.

Older children were now being urged with calls of "Come now, Michael! There's a good boy!" or "Do come, Elizabeth! We shall be late to tea!"

As that same evening approached, poor little Tom Jenks was growing more and more worried.

Many new guests had arrived that day and many errands had had to be run. Now it was six o'clock and he had not yet been able to leave and go back to Bob's hotel.

But at last he saw his chance and started off, thinking that his day's work was done.

As he neared the door, however, another page called after him that the manager desired to see him at once in his office!

Tom spent an unpleasant time with the manager, trying to explain why he had been late to work that morning. As punishment, the manager made him stay on that evening.

When he finally left, it was dark outside. This meant that it must be after nine o'clock, for in summer London remains light until about that hour.

Tom made up his mind to go to Bob's hotel, even though he was ready to drop with fatigue. Yes, he would go and see Bob Bentley tonight, even though his mother might worry.

But, of course, Tom did not see Bob, for he was told that the Bentleys had gone to the theatre.

So, knowing how concerned his family would be about him, Tom hurried home. He decided, however, to return to Bob's hotel in the morning.

Poor little Tom! Mrs. Bentley had also decided something. She had decided to leave London in the morning!

CHAPTER XIV

THE PARTING

Morning.

Bob and his mother were standing in the hotel lobby amidst a sea of luggage. They were waiting for the car to drive them to the airport. They were going to fly to Paris.

Bob was sorry to leave England. He felt that he had learned a great deal from his visit, not only about history and geography but about the English language!

He knew now that one must never ask in London for a "drug store." "Chemist" is the word. A radio, he discovered, is a "wireless"; an elevator, a "lift."

Oh, yes, he could almost say that he had learned a new language!

"The car is waiting, madam," said the doorman to Mrs. Bentley.

Their bags were put on a truck and
wheeled out. Bob followed his mother toward the revolving door and saw her
through. Then he himself stepped inside
the merry-go-round-like door.

Suddenly he gasped, for on the other side
of the glass door he had seen Tom Jenks!
Tom was entering the hotel!

But, as Tom stepped into the hotel lobby,
Bob stepped out into the street!

The American boy turned and banged on
the glass. "Oh, Tom!" he yelled.

Tom, inside, whirled around and saw Bob.

When his American friend rushed up
to him he smiled and breathed happily,
"Bob! I say!"

Bob's face was beaming. He wanted to
catch Tom's hand and give it a good shake.
He wanted— But wait! What he really
wanted to do was to knock Tom down! The
little thief! He had run off with Bob's
mother's locket!

BOB'S SMILE CHANGED TO A SCOWL

Bob's smile changed to a scowl. Tom saw and understood.

"Look here, Bob," he began, "I can explain, you know——"

But just at that moment Mrs. Bentley entered the lobby, looking very angry. The doorman had told her that he could not tear her son away from some "page person."

When Mrs. Bentley saw who the "page person" was, she hastened over eagerly to the two boys.

"Why, it's the little page from the ship!" she exclaimed. "I'm so glad you've come at last! And you've brought back my locket, haven't you?"

Tom drew something out of his pocket and started to speak to Mrs. Bentley, when the doorman appeared before them.

"Time to leave for the airport, madam," he said, "or I fear you'll miss your plane."

"We're coming," said Mrs. Bentley.

She had taken the locket from Tom and was looking at it with great relief in her face. She had, however, left the paper bills in his hand.

"You may keep the money, my boy," she said to him. "I am only glad that you decided at last to give up the locket."

"But madam—" Tom again tried to speak, but Mrs. Bentley interrupted him.

She laid a kindly hand on his shoulder. "It's all right, Tom," she smiled. "We won't say another word about it. Come, now, Bob. We really must go!"

"But Mrs. Bentley!" cried Tom.

Something desperate in the boy's voice made Mrs. Bentley turn.

"Please let me explain!" he pleaded. "It isn't at all what you think! I didn't keep your locket purposely! Really I didn't!"

The frantic appeal in his hurt, blue eyes touched Mrs. Bentley.

"Then come along to the airport with us and explain on the way," she said. "We're late now."

Tom did not hesitate. Forgetting that he had a job, which he would doubtless lose to-morrow, he rode off in the Bentleys' car.

And Tom did lose his job next day. But it really did not matter, because something very wonderful happened to the little page on that drive to the airport.

He explained all about the hole in his pocket and how, only the other night, his sister had found the locket and the money.

When he finished his story, Bob put out his hand and cried, "Gee! I'm glad, Tom! Now we can be friends again!"

This made Tom's dimple jump in and out joyfully.

Then Mrs. Bentley suddenly made a remark which so astonished the dimples that they entirely disappeared for a whole minute.

"How would you like to stop work and go to school, Tom?" was the remark she made.

"But—but—I—can't!" stammered Tom.

Mrs. Bentley seemed not to hear him. She went right on.

"How would you like it," she repeated, "if I sent you to school in England, just as I'm sending Bob to school in America?"

"But, my—my mother needs me," mumbled Tom.

"Let me take care of that, Tom," said
Mrs. Bentley kindly. "Bob and I are coming back to London soon and then I'll ar-
range it all. You see, I feel so grateful to
you for what you did for Bob."

"For—for Bob?" puzzled Tom. "Why, I
—I didn't do anything at all, you know!"

"Yes, you did," said Mrs. Bentley. "You
helped him to discover the joy there is in
learning."

Tom said nothing and Bob looked uncomfortable.

"Oliver Goldsmith once called England
the 'land of scholars,'" continued Mrs.
Bentley. "You are a scholar, Tom, and so
you shall go to the best schools and learn all
that you desire to learn!"

A teasing twinkle came into Bob's eye.
"And one day you'll become a great man!"
he said. "And my grandchildren will have
to study about you out of books!

"Why," he went on jestingly, "I'll be listening to your name on the radio—er—pardon me, I mean wireless. And I'll be seeing your face in the movies—er—I mean cinema. Gee, you'll be famous!"

Tom laughed and punched Bob. Bob punched back. Then they hit, wrestled and struggled until Mrs. Bentley and Harkness had to tear them apart when they reached the airport.

Bob's nose was bleeding and his tie was torn off. There were still one or two brass buttons left on Tom's uniform and his eye was swelling rapidly.

Oh, yes, the two little boys are terribly fond of each other. Yet Mrs. Bentley finds it a startling kind of love! Harkness, who has never been even a mother, finds it still more startling!

It comes time for the Bentleys' plane to leave. So Tom Jenks stands on the landing field, watching the flying ship rise off the ground.

Bob, waving from above, touches his nose, which is beginning to resemble a geranium. He grins. He has found a great pal!

Tom, waving from below, blinks his swelling eye, thinks of going to Oxford University some day, and blesses his American friends.

"So long!" calls Young America, from above.

"Cheerio!" shouts Young England, from below.

And the big, silver bird flies over the English Channel.

THE END

friends.

above.

below.

lish Channel.

THE END